For Rayne, Aurora, and Aria
—D.O'N.

For Topaz, Spirit, and Zena
—KM

STUBBORN GAL

the true story of an undefeated sled dog racer

Dan O'Neill
illustrated by Klara Maisch

University of Alaska Press Fairbanks

Grandpa, tell me a story about when you lived in Alaska.

All right. I'll tell you a story that happens to be true.

Once upon a time there was a young woman whose name was the same as yours: Sarah. This Sarah was tall and strong and pretty just like you. She lived in a cabin in the woods with her husband and their ten sled dogs.

One winter, Sarah's husband took a job for a few weeks in the oil fields way up north on the Arctic coast of Alaska. Sarah stayed home alone and kept the fire burning in the wood stove. Each day she took the dogs out for a run, five dogs at a time. In the evening she made up two buckets of food to feed the dogs.

One day, when she was bored at being home alone, she saw a small notice in the Fairbanks newspaper advertising two dog races, a 60-miler and a 30-miler.

"What the heck," thought Sarah, "I'll enter."

Sarah knew Andy Handwringer, one of the organizers, so she phoned him.

"I was thinking of entering that 60-mile race," Sarah said.
"Oh," said Andy, sounding surprised. "Not the 30-miler?"
"I was thinking the 60," said Sarah.
"Hmm," said Andy. "How many dogs would you run?"
"I guess I'd take all ten," she said.
"Gee, I'm not sure that would be such a good idea, Sarah," said Andy.
"Have you ever run ten dogs before?"
"No," she said.

THE DAILY NEWS
RACE ANNOUNCEMENT
A 60-mile and a 30 mile sled dog race will be held Saturday on the old freight trail between Fairbanks and Angel Creek Lodge. Call Aandy Handwringer or Burley Bob for information

It took plenty of strength to control even the five dogs she ran every day, each one weighing 50 to 60 pounds. She knew that a ten-dog team would be very powerful, and that it would take all her muscle and skill to control them.

"What if you fell off and the team got away?" asked Andy.

It's true, what Andy was getting at.

If a musher falls off the sled and loses the team, the dogs won't stop. They'll just run all the faster until they get into a big tangle somewhere down the trail. And that could lead to a terrible fight. It's very dangerous, no two ways about it. That's why a dog musher never lets go of the sled, even if it means dragging behind.

"I myself am going to run in the 30-miler," said Andy. "It will be easier and not really a race, but a 'fun run.' I think you should enter the 30-miler, Sarah, and with a smaller team. It really wouldn't be fair to the other mushers or to the dogs if you tried to run ten dogs and couldn't do it."

Did I mention that this Sarah was stubborn?

No.

Well, she was. Oh, boy!
Kind of quiet, but stubborn as a stump!
Sarah didn't argue with Andy.

But she didn't change her mind either.

The next morning she went out to the dog yard. As soon as she moved the sled, and its moosehide lashings started to squeak, every chain of every dog rattled across the threshold of every doghouse.

The yard buzzed with nervous energy. The dogs whizzed around their posts on the ends of their chains, whining and moaning.

They lunged, and the chains snapped taut.
They jumped up on their houses.
Then they jumped down again.

But when Sarah grabbed a harness and headed toward the first dog . . . why, the whole yard went completely nuts! Jumping jee-ackrabbits, what a racket! All the dogs braying and yapping until you couldn't hear yourself think!

I'll tell you right now, it's not easy to wrestle a powerful dog into a harness. Especially when it is squirming and struggling to break away and run off. That's another rule of dog mushing: never let go of the dog. One by one, Sarah danced the dogs over to the gangline and snapped them in place.

And don't think that a hitched up sled dog will stand still and wait like some old plow horse. No, ma'am! Sled dogs are "crazy to go," as the mushers say.

They'll bellow and yap and leap in the air.
They'll rear back and smash their shoulders into the harnesses.
And you're right to worry, too. Sometimes things break.
And if that happens . . . well, there goes the team without you!

But Sarah moved swiftly and surely and then hustled back onto the runners. It's pretty scary all right, with ten muscle-bound beasts screeching and slamming into their harnesses and the lines jerking tight as piano wires.

"Well, here goes," she thought, and yanked the slipknot.

The team shot ahead so fast it almost knocked Sarah over backwards! But she snatched the driving bow just in time and hung on for dear life. And at that moment . . . all the racket suddenly stopped. The dogs' frantic energy changed into power and speed. The only sound was the ssssshushing of the runners over the snow as the team burst out of the birch woods and charged into a big field.

Sarah leaned into the first turn, and the sled stayed upright. Now the trail turned down hill, and the team gathered even more speed. The temperature was twenty degrees below zero, with ice crystals in the air, and the freezing wind burned Sarah's face. She wanted to pull up her scarf to cover her nose, but she didn't dare take even one hand off the handlebar.

At the bottom of the hill the trail curved left, and Sarah leaned and skidded on the runners like you're supposed to do. But one runner slid off the hard-packed trail, and the sled tipped. WHOOSH!

She flew off like a missile, headfirst into a snowbank!

Pretty quick, the gangline went slack and the dogs piled up. Lines snaked every which way, and the more the dogs struggled, the more the lines tightened around their legs and necks. Sarah ran up to get the dogs apart before a fight broke out, but it was too late.

When a dog is pinched like that, he thinks another dog is biting him. So he snarls and bares his teeth and lashes out. A team can quickly turn into a giant ball of whirling fur and flashing fangs, all knotted together with ropes!

It's very dangerous.

Bravely—some might say "foolishly"—Sarah waded into the pile, unsnapping lines and throwing dogs apart while trying hard not to let her legs get tangled up in the lines. You don't want to fall down into a 500-pound heap of fighting dogs, that's for sure. As it was, reaching in among the snapping jaws, Sarah got her hand chomped good and hard.

It was all she could do to get the team back to the yard and the dogs chained up again. Inside the cabin, she doctored her bleeding hand and collapsed into a chair, totally exhausted.

The next day, with her hand bandaged and aching, Sarah loaded the eager dogs into the dog box, then drove down to the wide, frozen Tanana River. A stiff wind on the river made the temperature feel like twenty-five degrees below zero.

Her idea was to hook up the dogs right at the river's edge. She could tie the sled to the truck and hitch up the team all lined out at the edge of the long, straight river. The river had no hills or sharp turns to give her trouble. And once the dogs burned off their wild energy, they'd be more manageable. It was a good plan, but sometimes even good plans don't work out.

When Sarah pulled the slipknot, her leaders pulled a U-turn!

"No! No!" she yelled. But the dogs ignored her, and the sled flipped onto its side. With Sarah hanging on and dragging on her belly, the dogs took off across the icy parking lot at a full gallop.

Sarah hollered, "Whoa!" But the dogs kept going.

They ran right through the parking lot and straight across the highway, with Sarah bouncing through all the bumps and potholes. If a car had been coming down the road, Sarah and the dogs could easily have been run over and killed. It's happened before.

Instead, our gal ended up battered and bruised in the far side ditch,
with the dogs all tangled up in the willows.

The next day was the day of the race.
And what do you suppose this Sarah did?

She went to the race?

Exactly.
She loaded up the dogs and drove to the start of the 60-miler.
Not the 30-miler. She was that stubborn.

Or that bold.

Everybody figured that Burly Bob would win.

Bob was a big fellow with a square jaw, and he won lots of races in Fairbanks. Plus, Bob had cut most of the trail for the race and trained his dogs on it. Yup, Bob was almost certain to win, and the certainest person of all was Burly Bob.

The trail out to the finish line at Angel Creek Lodge started on a slough, then ran on the Chena River, then along the old freight trail, then on a borrowed bit of somebody's trapline, then back on the river—in other words, it was a total mish-mash and hard to follow. Burly Bob agreed to go first because he was the only one who knew exactly where it went. That way, the following teams' lead dogs could smell which way to go at each fork.

Bob took off with 12 strong dogs. Another 11 teams left every five minutes. There were good mushers in the lineup too, including several Iditarod racers. Sarah drew seventh position. Good thing there were lots of handlers there who could keep her team under control.

Just before the countdown for Sarah to go, her husband showed up.
He'd driven down from the Arctic and arrived just in time
to see her get off to a clean start.

START

‹ed and fast, and Sarah passed several teams.
‹y and slow. Burly Bob stopped sometimes to give
pectators. But pretty soon he'd pull the hook.

Don't want to lose my own race," he'd say.

As the hours went by, the trail got even more difficult, and when night fell the temperature dropped below zero. Sarah pulled up her hood and switched on her headlamp. Eventually she found herself way up a hillside on a tiny trail that made crazy turns through the spruce trees. It looked like no one had passed over this trail in weeks.

She must have taken a wrong turn.
She didn't know where she was and began apologizing to the dogs.
"You guys did so well.
I'm sorry I let you down."

7

A nearly full moon had risen when Sarah finally popped out of the woods onto the bank of the Chena River. And there was her husband standing there.

"Wow! I'm not lost?" she asked.
"Nope," he said. He pointed up the river, "Haw at the bend."
A dog musher says "haw" to get the dogs to turn left,
and "gee" to get them to turn right.

7

A few minutes later, up at Angel Creek Lodge, someone poked his head into the bar and shouted, "Musher coming! I can see a headlight!" The crowd boiled out of the lodge. It was Burly Bob, the first to cross the finish line and grinning from ear to ear.

"Didn't hardly feel like a race," he crowed.
"Never saw another team all day long!"

People slapped the champ's back and shook his hand. Burly mugged for a few pictures and allowed that, yeah, he'd expected to win all right.

ANGEL CREEK
OPEN
1
RACE
OFFICIAL

Bob and his pals headed into the lodge—Bob to get his dogs some water, the others to get themselves some refreshment. Among them was Andy Handwringer, who'd finished the 30-mile race earlier in the day. When Andy saw Sarah's husband over by the dog trucks he went over to him. With a worried look and a bit of I-told-you-so in his voice, he asked, "Do you think she'll be all right out there?"

"Well, I guess so," said Sarah's husband, nodding toward the finish line. "I believe she's just won this race."

Andy spun around to look, and sure enough, there was Sarah's team pulling in out of the night and into the glow of the yard lights. She'd started the race 30 minutes after Burly Bob, but finished only eight minutes after him.

Her time was faster by 22 minutes!

1

What a party at the lodge that night! Man alive! Music blaring, everybody in their shoepacs and coveralls whooping it up. First prize was a plaque and a case of, er, root beer, I think it was. Sarah tore open the case and gave her winnings away.

It took Burly Bob a while to get over the shock of losing . . . especially to a rookie . . . and even more especially to a girl! But after a while (and after a couple of root beers) the best sport of all was Burly Bob. He made jokes, telling everyone, “I had a place on my wall picked out for that plaque. Heck, I already drove in the nail!”

As for Sarah, she thought it was fun to race and fun to win. But mainly she was just happy to finish something she set out to do—especially when people thought she couldn’t do it. And once was enough. She never entered another race, which might make her the only undefeated dog racer in Alaska history!

Grandpa?

Yeah?

Did you know that other Sarah?

Well, I guess so.
And so do you.

The events in this book actually happened.

In the winter of 1981, a young woman named **Sarah** from Fairbanks, Alaska, entered a 60-mile sled dog race. She had never run in a race before, never run a big string of dogs, and had been strongly discouraged from entering. She had all the difficulties described here, and more. But she persisted and won. It was her only race. She has a granddaughter named Sarah.

Dan O'Neill moved from his native San Francisco to Fairbanks, Alaska, in 1975. In Fairbanks he mushed dogs, produced radio and television documentaries, authored three books of adult nonfiction, and was named Alaska Historian of the Year in 1994. He has a wife, a son, and three granddaughters.

Klara Maisch is a Fairbanks-born artist who graduated from the University of Alaska Fairbanks with a degree in fine art. She has won numerous grants and scholarships, and through the Artists-in-Schools Program, has produced exciting and colorful murals for children. Klara learned to mush dogs at a young age from her friend Willa and Willa's dad Bill. This is the first book she has illustrated.

Published June 2015 by
University of Alaska Press
P.O. Box 756240
Fairbanks, AK 99775-6240

Library of Congress Cataloging-in-Publication Data
O'Neill, Dan (Daniel T.).
Stubborn gal : the true story of an undefeated sled dog racer / by Dan O'Neill ; illustrated by Klara Maisch.
pages cm
ISBN 978-1-60223-272-3 (pbk. : alk. paper)
1. Sled dog racing--Alaska--Juvenile literature. 2. Mushers--Alaska--Juvenile literature. 3. Women mushers--Alaska--Juvenile literature. I. Maisch, Klara. II. Title.
SF440.15.O54 2015
798.8'309798--dc23
2014050118

Cover and interior design by Krista West
Illustrations by Klara Maisch

This publication was printed on acid-free paper that meets the minimum requirements for ANSI / NISO Z39.48—1992 (R2002) (Permanence of Paper for Printed Library Materials).

Printed in China by Four Colour Print Group, Louisville, Kentucky
Batch 767673